EASTER
ACTIVITY BOOK

This Book Belongs To:

_____

Bunny Maze

Help the bunny get his egg to the basket.

I Spy

Can you count all the eggs?

Odd One Out

Can you find the odd ones out in this puzzle?

A   B   C   D

A   B   C   D

A   B   C   D

Match The Pair

Which baskets do you think go together?

Crack The Code

Why was the Easter egg hiding?

Crack the code to find the answer.

	1	2	3	4	5
A	WAS	BUNNY	BASKET	PINK	PLANTS
B	YELLOW	BUTTERFLY	A	IT	FLOWER
C	SPRING	BECAUSE	GREEN	PURPLE	ORANGE
D	CHICK	EGGS	CHICKEN	BLUE	LITTLE

1

_____ _____ _____ _____
C2   B4   A1   B3

_____ _____
D5   D3

Word Maze

Follow the word SPRING twice to complete the maze.

Crossword

Solve the crossword with the words below.

BUNNY BUTTERFLY FLOWER

BASKET SPRING LADYBUGS

Find The Difference

Find the 5 differences in the pictures below.

Word Search

Can you find all the words below?

```
W R G Q A P V R F P N J
P G B U N N Y I A C M M
K C K Z Z W V Q E G G S
F O C H I C K Y J A D N
I E A S T E R R N N W H
S F B C H O C O L A T E
F N B Z N U C M E D Y S
H E A X V K A O K Y T A
Q Y S R D P N T H E I X
Q H K R J P D S F Y V Z
K J E M X P Y V E Z F Q
K A T U S N X Z J I V B
```

BUNNY	CHICK	CHOCOLATE	CANDY
EGGS	EASTER	BASKET	DYE

Two of a Kind

Can you find the two identical eggs?

Dot To Dot

Join the dots to complete the picture.

1
2
3
4
5
6
7
8
9
10
11
12
13
14
15

Word Maze

Follow the word GARDEN twice to complete the maze.

Hidden Items

Find the hidden items in the picture.

What Doesn't Belong

Can you find the five things that
don't belong in the scene?

Word Search

Can you find all the words below?

```
C B D O N S W E M G H T
J E L L Y B E A N R O Z
I P I B N L M M L A D C
B K H B E D D Q H S P Z
P Y O S U N D A Y S X P
J S P I J A T N X Y U I
S P L A M B Y I Z Y G Q
D R U F O P F L O W E R
C I D U C K G H A I O N
B N L V X S P N U H F T
P G M G J U M M X L H C
R P E E P S I K F T P O
```

JELLYBEAN	SUNDAY	LAMB	PEEPS
GRASS	SPRING	DUCK	FLOWER

What Am I?

Can you name these Easter items below?

Finish The Picture

Finish drawing the bunny below.

Word Scramble

Descramble the words on the baskets.

YACDN

STEARE

SUNBIEN

DGHINI

What Doesn't Belong?

Find the odd one out in each group.

Spot The Difference

Can you find the 6 differences in the picture?

Sudoku

Fill in the blank squares so that numbers 1 to 6 appear once in each row, column, and box.

	6			3	2
3	2		5	1	
			2		3
		6	1		4
6	1			4	
		3		2	

Crack The Code

Solve the puzzles to answer the riddle.

1 x 2 = _____ ⓐ   3 x 2 = _____ ⓟ

3 ÷ 3 = _____ ⓗ   10 ÷ 2 = _____ ⓒ

8 - 5 = _____ ⓢ   10 - 1 = _____ ⓔ

12 + 8 = _____ ⓘ   17 + 1 = _____ ⓦ

6 x 2 = _____ ⓚ   4 x 2 = _____ ⓣ

8 ÷ 2 = _____ ⓥ   10 + 1 = _____ ⓝ

20 - 10 = _____ ⓖ   15 - 8 = _____ ⓧ

18 + 1= _____ ⓤ   11 + 3 = _____ ⓠ

Why did the duck get fired from his Easter job?

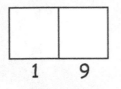

  1 9

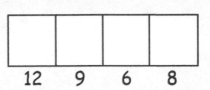

  12 9 6 8

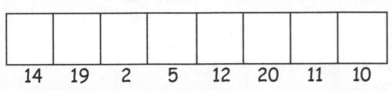

14 19 2 5 12 20 11 10

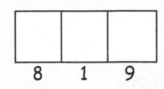

8 1 9

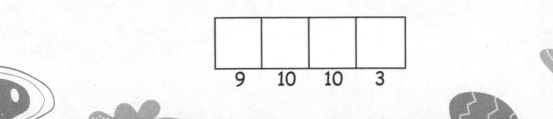

  9 10 10 3

Egg Maze

Help the chick get through the maze to the egg.

Word Scramble

Descramble the words on these eggs.

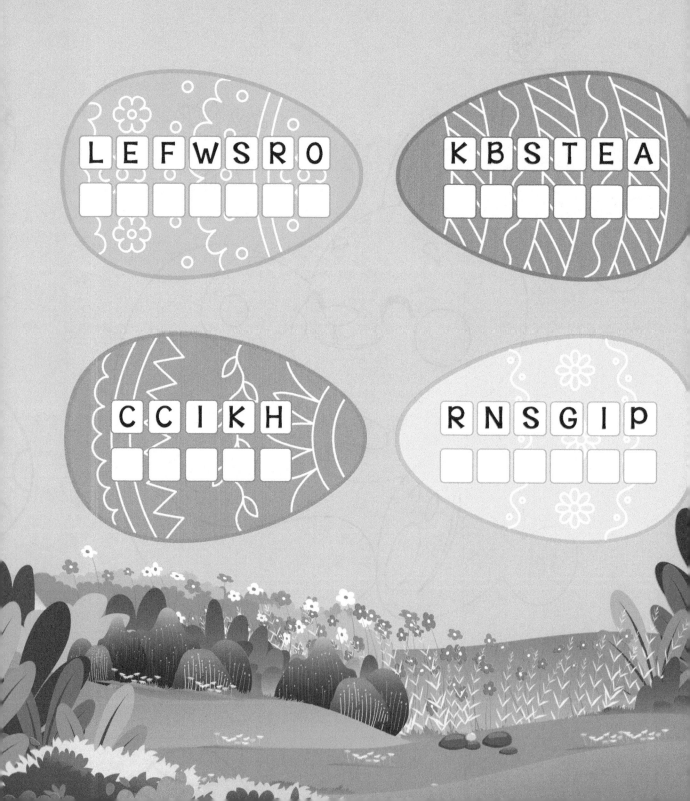

LEFWSRO

KBSTEA

CCIKH

RNSGIP

Look And find

Count the objects in the picture.

Decorate the Eggs

Jazz up these eggs with your own cool patterns!

Finish The Puzzle

Finish the puzzle with the missing pieces.

a.

b.

c.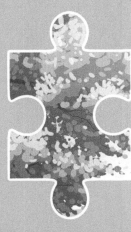

Match The Shadow

Match the object to the correct shadow.

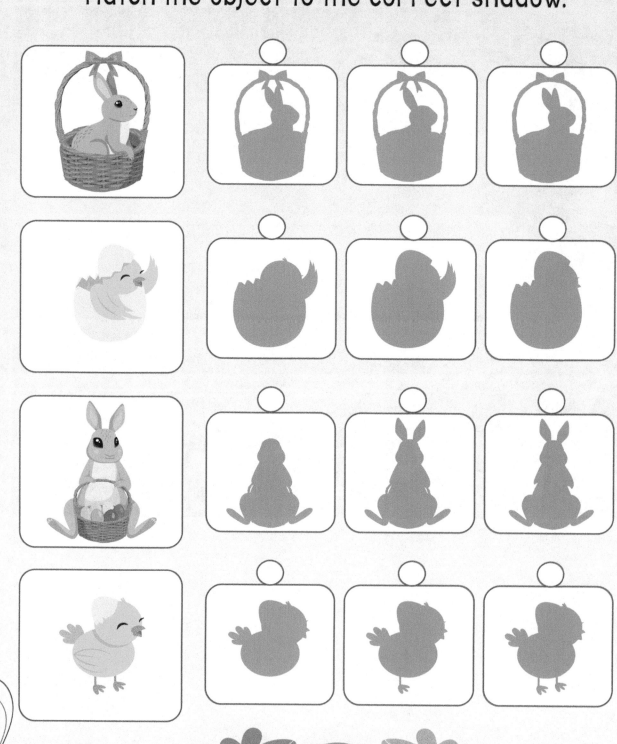

Word Search

Find all the words in the puzzle below.

```
U G A M E S U J T U F U
E L R L X Q A Z Z G T N
D F U H I D E G Q T P J
H P T Q V U S C C P A N
U R A B B I T E T F R T
N S C M H A T C Y F A U
T X A J T R G N M L D L
S G R I U T H V J B E I
G X R F Y M V L I L Y P
W I O Z N C Z K L H O X
K D T F P P A S T E L A
I W J J E D N R J K X F
```

GAMES	HIDE	CARROT	PASTEL	HAT
HUNT	RABBIT	LILLY	TULIP	PARADE

Finish The Picture

Finish drawing the bunny and his backpack of eggs.

Sudoku

Fill in the blank squares so that numbers 1 to 6 appear once in each row, column, and box.

3	6			2	5
		4			
4	2	3		5	
	1	5			
5	4	6	2		3
		2	5		

Crack The Code

What's the best way to catch a rabbit?

Crack the code to find the answer.

	1	2	3	4	5
A	BUNNIES	MEADOW	PINK	FLOWER	ARE
B	A	BUTTERFLY	PRETEND	PASTEL	SPRING
C	GREEN	TULIP	LADYBUG	HUNT	BASKET
D	YOU	HIDE	CHOCOLATE	CHICKS	CARROT

1

_____   _____   _____
   B3   D1   A5

_____   _____
   B1   D5

Find Hidden Items

Find the hidden objects in the picture below.

Tally o Graph

Can you count the objects correctly?

Count and write.

Circle according to the items counted.

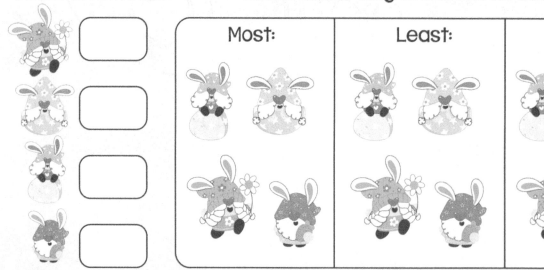

Most:	Least:	Same:

Match The Shadow

Match the object to the correct shadow.

What Am I?

Can you name all these items found in a garden?

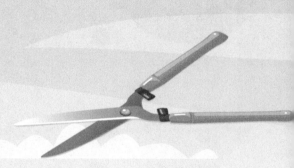

Gnome Maze

Can you help the Gnome reach his friend?

Match The Pair

Can you match the pairs of Gnomes?

Dot To Dot

Join the dots to complete the picture.

Crossword

Fill in the words to solve the puzzle.

Word Search

Can you find all the words below?

```
G R L F A M I L Y G A U
I S P L V Z B O N N E T
P W G E H B D L H V V D
R E Q A A P R C O M X R
F E K R H O P V L L B W
I T D S T D F G I B C F
N S M N Y I B X D L A A
D K B L O O M S A Z K X
K X F N L S Y Y Y W E T
Q L R V M T T L L G R J
O P W F M E N K C D M H
P H I D E E X E H G C M
```

BLOOMS	SWEETS	HOP	FAMILY	FIND
HIDE	BONNET	CAKE	HOLIDAY	EARS

Find Hidden Items

Find the hidden objects in the picture below.

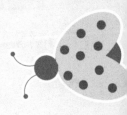

Draw A Scene

Draw your favorite Easter scene.

Sudoku

Fill in the blank squares so that numbers 1 to 6 appear once in each row, column, and box.

6	4	2	1		3
	5	1			4
2			4		
1	3	4		2	5
4	2				6
5	1		3	4	

Match The Shadow

Match the object to the correct shadow.

Finish The Puzzle

Finish the puzzle with the missing pieces.

a.

b.

c.

Two of a Kind

Can you find the two identical gnomes?

ANSWER KEY

Bunny Maze
Help the bunny get his egg to the basket.

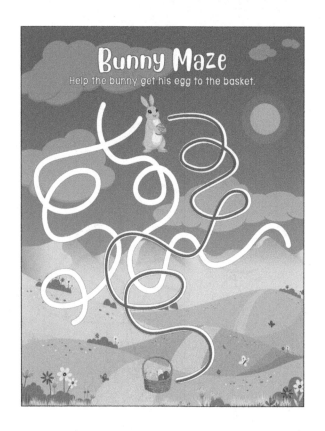

I SPY
Can you count all the eggs?

Odd One Out
Can you find the odd ones out in this puzzle?

Match The Pair
Which baskets do you think go together?

ANSWER KEY

Crack The Code

Why was the Easter egg hiding?
Crack the code to find the answer.

	1	2	3	4	5
A	WAS	BUNNY	BASKET	PINK	PLANTS
B	YELLOW	BUTTERFLY	A	IT	FLOWER
C	SPRING	BECAUSE	GREEN	PURPLE	ORANGE
D	CHICK	EGGS	CHICKEN	BLUE	LITTLE

①

BECAUSE	IT	WAS	A
C2	B4	A1	B3
	LITTLE	CHICKEN	
	D5	D3	

Word Maze
Follow the word SPRING twice to complete the maze.

Crossword
Solve the crossword with the words below.

BUNNY
BUTTERFLY
FLOWER

BASKET
SPRING
LADYBUGS

Find The Difference
Find the 5 differences in the pictures below.

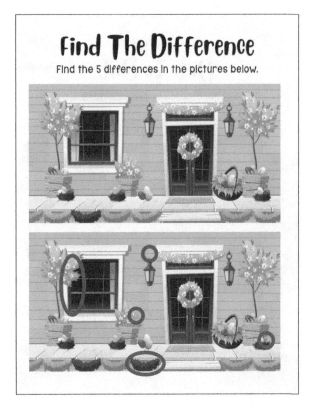

ANSWER KEY

Word Search
Can you find all the words below?

W	R	G	Q	A	P	V	R	F	P	N	J
P	G	B	U	N	N	Y	I	A	C	M	M
K	C	K	Z	Z	W	V	Q	E	G	G	S
F	O	C	H	I	C	K	Y	J	A	D	N
I	E	A	S	T	E	R	R	N	N	W	H
S	F	B	C	H	O	C	O	L	A	T	E
F	N	B	Z	N	U	C	M	E	D	Y	S
H	E	A	X	V	K	A	O	K	Y	T	A
Q	Y	S	R	D	P	N	T	H	E	I	X
Q	H	K	R	J	P	D	S	F	Y	V	Z
K	J	E	M	X	P	Y	V	E	Z	F	Q
K	A	T	U	S	N	X	Z	J	I	V	B

BUNNY   CHICK   CHOCOLATE   CANDY

EGGS   EASTER   BASKET   DYE

Two of a Kind
Can you find the two identical eggs?

Dot To Dot
Join the dots to complete the picture.

Word Maze
Follow the word GARDEN twice to complete the maze.

ANSWER KEY

Hidden Items
Find the hidden items in the picture.

What Doesn't Belong
Can you find the five things that don't belong in the scene?

Word Search
Can you find all the words below?

C	B	D	O	N	S	W	E	M	G	H	T
J	E	L	L	Y	B	E	A	N	R	O	Z
I	P	I	B	N	L	M	M	L	A	D	C
B	K	H	B	E	D	D	Q	H	S	P	Z
P	Y	O	S	U	N	D	A	Y	S	X	P
J	S	P	I	J	A	T	N	X	Y	U	I
S	P	L	A	M	B	Y	I	Z	Y	G	Q
D	R	U	F	O	P	F	L	O	W	E	R
C	I	D	U	C	K	G	H	A	I	O	N
B	N	L	V	X	S	P	N	U	H	F	T
P	G	M	G	J	U	M	M	X	L	H	C
R	P	E	E	P	S	I	K	F	T	P	O

JELLYBEAN	SUNDAY	LAMB	PEEPS
GRASS	SPRING	DUCK	FLOWER

What Am I?
Can you name these Easter items below?

BASKET   EGGS

BUNNY   CHICK

ANSWER KEY

Finish The Picture

Finish drawing the bunny below.

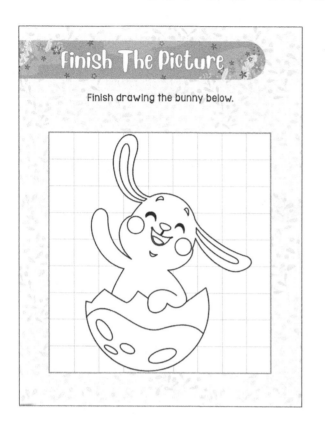

Word Scramble

Descramble the words on the baskets.

YACDN — CANDY

STEARE — EASTER

SUNBIEN — BUNNIES

DGHINI — HIDING

What Doesn't Belong?

Find the odd one out in each group.

Spot The Difference

Can you find the 6 differences in the picture?

ANSWER KEY

Sudoku

Fill in the blank squares so that numbers 1 to 6 appear once in each row, column, and box.

5	6	1	4	3	2
3	2	4	5	1	6
1	4	5	2	6	3
2	3	6	1	5	4
6	1	2	3	4	5
4	5	3	6	2	1

Crack The Code

Solve the puzzles to answer the riddle.

1 x 2 =	2	a
3 ÷ 3 =	1	h
8 - 5 =	3	s
12 + 8 =	20	l
6 x 2 =	12	k
8 ÷ 2 =	4	v
20 - 10 =	10	g
18 + 1=	19	u

3 x 2 =	6	p
10 ÷ 2 =	5	c
10 - 1 =	9	e
17 + 1 =	18	w
4 x 2 =	8	t
10 + 1 =	11	n
15 - 8 =	7	x
11 + 3 =	14	q

Why did the duck get fired from his Easter job?

h	e		k	e	p	t
1	9		12	9	6	8

q	u	a	c	k	i	n	g		t	h	e
14	19	2	5	12	20	11	10		8	1	9

e	g	g	s
9	10	10	3

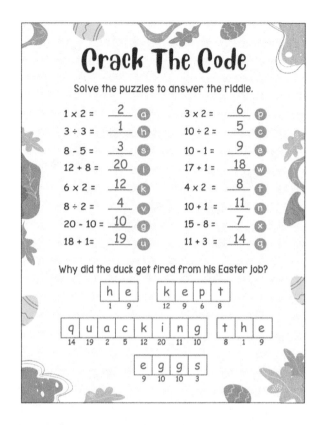

Egg Maze

Help the chick get through the maze to the egg.

Word Scramble

Descramble the words on these eggs.

LEFWSRO → FLOWERS

KBSTEA → BASKET

CCIKH → CHICK

RNSGIP → SPRING

ANSWER KEY

Look And find
Count the objects in the picture.

🌷	12	🥚	7	🐞	21
🥜	16	🌿	6	🪺	4

Finish The Puzzle
Finish the puzzle with the missing pieces.

a.   b.   c.

Match The Shadow
Match the object to the correct shadow.

Word Search
Find all the words in the puzzle below.

U	G	A	M	E	S	U	J	T	U	F	U
E	L	R	L	X	Q	A	Z	Z	G	T	N
D	F	U	H	I	D	E	G	Q	T	P	J
H	P	T	Q	V	U	S	C	C	P	A	N
U	R	A	B	B	I	T	E	T	F	R	T
N	S	C	M	H	A	T	C	Y	F	A	U
T	X	A	J	T	R	G	N	M	L	D	L
S	G	R	I	U	T	H	V	J	B	E	I
G	X	R	F	Y	M	V	L	I	L	Y	P
W	I	O	Z	N	C	Z	K	L	H	O	X
K	D	T	F	P	P	A	S	T	E	L	A
I	W	J	J	E	D	N	R	J	K	X	F

GAMES	HIDE	CARROT	PASTEL	HAT
HUNT	RABBIT	LILLY	TULIP	PARADE

ANSWER KEY

Finish The Picture

Finish drawing the bunny and his backpack of eggs.

Sudoku

Fill in the blank squares so that numbers 1 to 6 appear once in each row, column, and box.

3	6	1	4	2	5
2	5	4	6	3	1
4	2	3	1	5	6
6	1	5	3	4	2
5	4	6	2	1	3
1	3	2	5	6	4

Crack The Code

What's the best way to catch a rabbit?

Crack the code to find the answer.

	1	2	3	4	5
A	BUNNIES	MEADOW	PINK	FLOWER	ARE
B	A	BUTTERFLY	PRETEND	PASTEL	SPRING
C	GREEN	TULIP	LADYBUG	HUNT	BASKET
D	YOU	HIDE	CHOCOLATE	CHICKS	CARROT

1.

PRETEND	YOU	ARE
B3	D1	A5

A	CARROT
B1	D5

Find Hidden Items

Find the hidden objects in the picture below.

ANSWER KEY

Tally o Graph

Can you count the objects correctly?

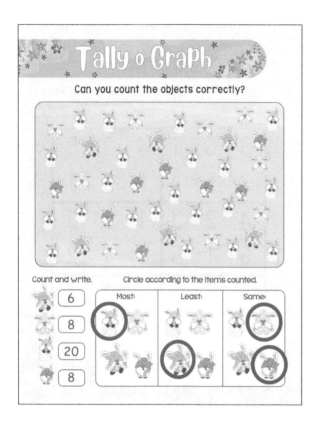

Count and write.

6
8
20
8

Circle according to the items counted.

Most:
Least:
Same:

Match The Shadow

Match the object to the correct shadow.

What Am I?

Can you name all these items found in a garden?

PLANT

CLIPPERS

WATERING CAN

TROWEL

Gnome Maze

Can you help the Gnome reach his friend?

ANSWER KEY

Match The Pair
Can you match the pairs of Gnomes?

Dot To Dot
Join the dots to complete the picture.

Crossword
Fill in the words to solve the puzzle.

TULIP
CANDY
CARROTS
GRASS
CHICK
JELLYBEAN

Word Search
Can you find all the words below?

G	R	L	F	A	M	I	L	Y	G	A	U
I	S	P	L	V	Z	B	O	N	N	E	T
P	W	G	E	H	B	D	L	H	V	V	D
R	E	Q	A	A	P	R	C	O	M	X	R
F	E	K	R	H	O	P	V	L	L	B	W
I	T	D	S	T	D	F	G	I	B	C	F
N	S	M	N	Y	I	B	X	D	L	A	A
D	K	B	L	O	O	M	S	A	Z	K	X
K	X	F	N	L	S	Y	Y	Y	W	E	T
Q	L	R	V	M	T	T	L	L	G	R	J
O	P	W	F	M	E	N	K	C	D	M	H
P	H	I	D	E	E	X	E	H	G	C	M

| BLOOMS | SWEETS | HOP | FAMILY | FIND |
| HIDE | BONNET | CAKE | HOLIDAY | EARS |

ANSWER KEY

Find Hidden Items

Find the hidden objects in the picture below.

Sudoku

Fill in the blank squares so that numbers 1 to 6 appear once in each row, column, and box.

6	4	2	1	5	3
3	5	1	2	6	4
2	6	5	4	3	1
1	3	4	6	2	5
4	2	3	5	1	6
5	1	6	3	4	2

Match The Shadow

Match the object to the correct shadow.

Finish The Puzzle

Finish the puzzle with the missing pieces.

a.　b.　c.

ANSWER KEY

Two of a Kind

Can you find the two identical gnomes?

Made in the USA
Las Vegas, NV
12 March 2023

68933261R00044